Atheneum
Books for Young Readers
1230 Avenue of the Americas   New
York, New York 10020   Copyright © 2001
by Viacom International Inc.   Nickelodeon,
Oswald, and all related titles, logos, and characters are
trademarks of Viacom International Inc.   All rights
reserved, including the right of reproduction in whole or in
part in any form.   Book design by Michael Nelson   The text
of this book is set in Humanist 521BT.   The illustrations are
rendered digitally.   Printed in Hong Kong
2   4   6   8   10   9   7   5   3   1
Library of Congress Cataloging-in-Publication Data:
Yaccarino, Dan.   Oswald / Dan Yaccarino.   p.   cm. Summary:
Oswald the Octopus and his dog, Weenie, make
many new friends when they move to Big City.
ISBN 0-689-84252-X   [1. Octopus—Fiction. 2. Dogs—
Fiction. 3. Moving, Household—Fiction.]   I. Title.
PZ7.Y125 Os 2001   [E]dc21   00-056572
A BIG THANKS TO ANTOINE GUILBAUD
FOR ALL OF HIS GOOD WORK.
—D. Y.

FIRST
EDITION

OSWALD

Dan Yaccarino

ATHENEUM BOOKS for YOUNG READERS
New York London Toronto Sydney Singapore

Oswald the Octopus and his pet hot dog, Weenie, were about to begin a big adventure in Big City.

"Gosh," said Oswald. "I sure am excited about moving to a new home in a new city, but I'm afraid I don't have any friends here."

"Bark! Bark!" replied Weenie. She knew that Oswald was a friendly fellow and would make lots and lots of new friends in no time at all.

"Here we are, girl," said Oswald.

The first thing Oswald wanted to move into his new home was his piano. It was his most favorite thing of all.

"**Umph, umph,**" said Oswald as he pushed the heavy piano.

"**Umph, umph,**" he said again. It wouldn't budge. Not one bit.

"**Bark! Bark!**" said Weenie. And she helped push, too. That did the trick.

Oswald and Weenie had quite a time getting
that piano up the stairs.
They stopped for a moment to take a rest.

"**Whew!**" said Oswald as he caught his breath.

"**Creak!**" said the stairs as the piano started to roll down them.

"**Bark!**" said Weenie as she jumped out of the way.

"**Splinkie, splinkie, splinkie,**" said the piano as it rolled down the sidewalk.

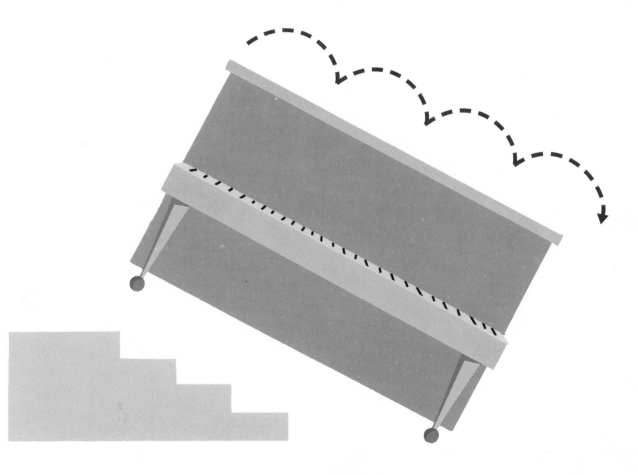

Oswald tried his best to stop the runaway piano.
Weenie bark-bark-barked all the way down the
street after him.

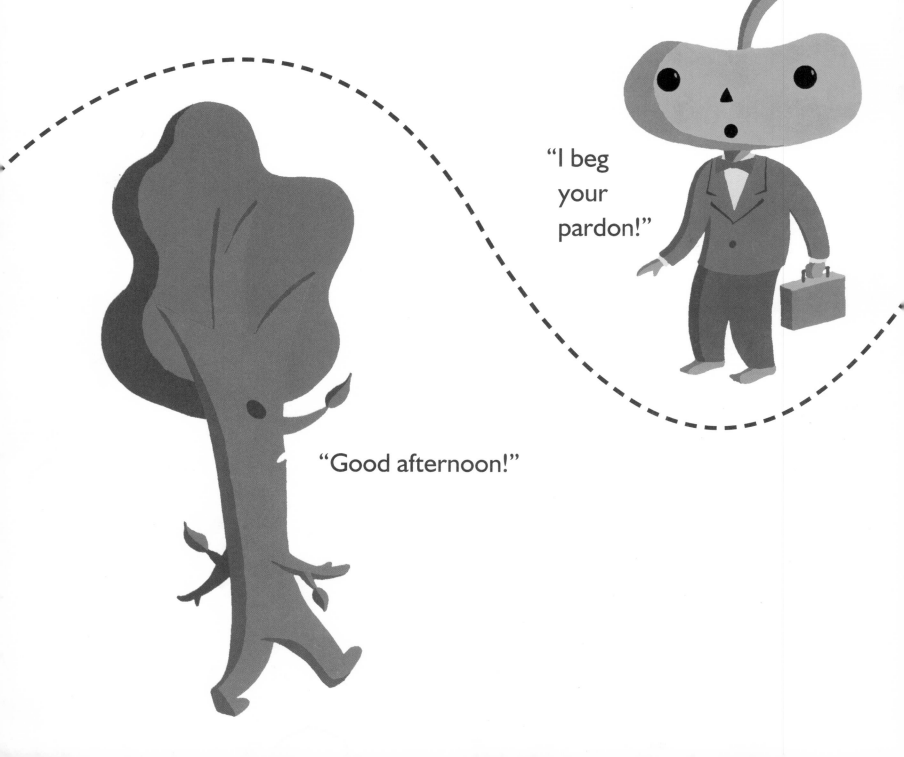

"I beg
your
pardon!"

"Good afternoon!"

"Splinkie, splinkie, splinkie."

Just then, a penguin walked up to Oswald.
"I'm Henry," he said. "Say, don't you think
it's a little chilly for swimming?"

Oswald explained that he was new in town and was trying to move his piano into his new home and—

"Say no more," interrupted Henry. "I'd be glad to lend a hand."

"**Umph, umph,**" said Oswald.
"**Bark! Bark!**" said Weenie.
"**A little to the left,**" said Henry.

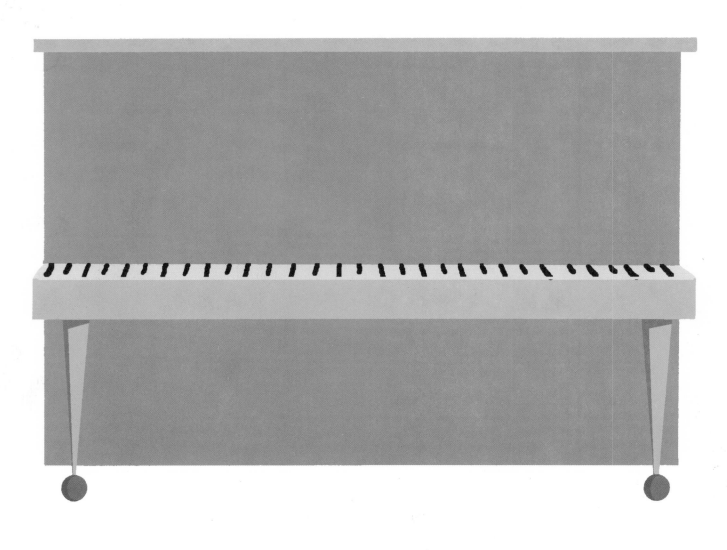

"Well, howdy-do, Henry! Who are your friends?" asked a daisy named Daisy.

Henry introduced Oswald and Weenie to Daisy. Oswald explained that they were new in town and were trying to move his piano into his new home.

"Need some help?" Daisy asked.
They certainly did.
   "Umph, umph," said Oswald.
   "Bark! Bark!" said Weenie.
   "Hoo-wee," said Daisy.
   "Are we there yet?"
asked Henry.

After all that pushing, Oswald, Weenie, Daisy, and even Henry were quite tired.

"How about some snowcones? My treat!" said Oswald.

"Yippity skippity!" said Daisy.

"Bark! Bark!" said Weenie.

"Make mine a sardine swirl," said Henry.

Oswald ordered snowcones—one for everybody.

"Hi, I'm Johnny. You're new around here, aren't you?" asked the snowman behind the counter.

"Yes," Oswald replied. He told Johnny Snowman that he was new in town and was trying to move his piano into his new home.

"Well, I'd be mighty glad to help," said Johnny Snowman.

And so he did.

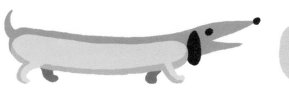

"Umph, umph," said Oswald.
"Bark! Bark!" said Weenie.
"Hoo-wee," said Daisy.
"Whew," said Johnny.
"Can't you push any faster?" said Henry.

Soon, they needed another rest.

Oswald entertained everyone with a little song. Johnny
Snowman snapped his fingers, Daisy clapped her hands,
Weenie tapped her foot, and Henry shook his tail feathers.

In the middle of all of this
snapping, clapping, tapping, and
shaking, the Egg Twins, Egbert
and his brother Leo, strolled by.
    "Good heavens!" said Egbert.
"What's all this?"
    "Yes! Yes!" said Leo. "Good
heavens!"

Oswald explained that he was new in town and
was trying to move his piano into his new home.
The Egg Twins offered their services as top-notch
piano pushers.

"Umph, umph," said Oswald.

"Bark! Bark!" said Weenie.

"Hoo-wee," said Daisy.

"Whew," said Johnny.

"Heave," said Egbert.

"Ho," said Leo.

**"Say, could we stop at the diner?
I'd like to get a muffin,"** said Henry.

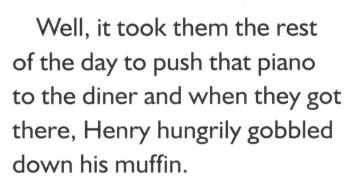

Well, it took them the rest of the day to push that piano to the diner and when they got there, Henry hungrily gobbled down his muffin.

"My stars!" said Madame Butterfly, the owner of the diner. "What is this? A parade?"

"Gurgle, gurgle," said her daughter, Catrina Caterpillar.

Oswald explained that he was new in town and was trying to move his piano into his new home.

"That's all well and good," Madame Butterfly said, "but when all that piano pushing is done you will certainly be hungry. I'd better come with you."

Everyone agreed, especially Henry. Quick as a wink, she brought out more cakes and pies than Oswald had ever seen, and followed along.

"**Umph, umph,**" said Oswald.

"**Bark! Bark!**" said Weenie.

"**Hoo-wee,**" said Daisy.

"**Whew,**" said Johnny.

"**Heave,**" said Egbert.

"**Ho,**" said Leo.

"**Oh my,**" said Madame Butterfly.
"**Gubba, gubba,**" said Catrina Caterpillar.
"**Yawn,**" said Henry.

In no time they were at Oswald's new home and his piano was in place. Everyone pitched in and moved the rest of his things as well.

"Who wants some pie?" asked Madame Butterfly.

Everyone had a piece. Henry had two. Oswald played his piano and everyone danced.

"Bark! Bark!" said Weenie. She knew that Oswald was a friendly
fellow and would make lots and lots of new friends in no time at all.